HOW TO BE KIND

Book I in The Art of a Messy House series

Written by Jennifer Kosuda

Illustrated by Courtney Monday

For TJ and Madison - May you always follow the plan God has for your life. - JK

Copyright © 2020 by Jennifer Kosuda

Book 1 of The Art of a Messy House series

All rights reserved. No part of this book may be reproduced in any form on or by an electronic or mechanical means, including information storage and retrieval systems, without permission in writing from the publisher, except by a reviewer who may quote brief passages in a review.

Illustrated by Courtney Monday

Scripture taken from the International Children's Bible®.
Copyright © 2015 by Thomas Nelson. Used by permission. All rights reserved.

ISBN: 978-1-7362182-0-4

Come along with Timothy and his sister Madison
with their stuffed buddies Courage and Hope by their sides,
and walk with them as they learn
that God always provides.

For no matter what we face
God is by our side.
So sit back and read,
learn His faithful words,
and let them lead the way
on this imperfectly beautiful ride.

Messy House logo illustrated by Kim King

No matter what day it is,
there is so much to learn.
From day one,
Timothy and Joshua learn that for some people,
it is not always easy to wait their turn.

This is when Asher cuts in
and steals the new student's spot,
but no one says anything to help Seth out
because Asher makes fun of a lot.

So they avoid
and sometimes pretend not to see,
but that is not the way
God wants us to be.

That night both Timothy and Joshua go home
and reflect on the day.
They know in their hearts
that speaking up against what is wrong
is the best way.

For when someone becomes cruel
and takes it out on someone new,
just know that being a kind friend
starts with...

So the next day
when Asher tried to get his way...

That is all that was needed
for the teacher to see.

So stand up for what is right
no matter who is the biggest in the smallest crowd.
They may shout back with mean words,
but always remember,
kindness can be just as loud.

Being a friend is being kind to all
because kindness is love,
and love is
the greatest gift of them all.

Bedtime Reflection

Courage is Timothy's dinosaur
and Hope is his sister's colorful friend.
They go along with them on daily adventures,
and find each other at the day's end.

Both furry buddies like to talk,
and reflect on the day before bed.
So after that day at school,
here is what they said.

For The Whole Family

Dear God,

Thank you for your love and how you write the lyrics to my daily song,
for even when I feel weak, you are making me strong.
Forgive me when I fail to do what is right
but help me now think of others and become an upstander,
shining your light.
For patience and kindness are both worth it, and they help us rise above
especially when each day ends in cuddles, smiles and love.
In Jesus' name,
Amen.

There's more truth where that came from in the Bible.

★ 1 Corinthians 13:4,13 ICB
★ Galatians 6:10 ICB
★ 1 John 3:18 ICB

"Love is patient and kind...So these three things continue forever: faith, hope and love."
(1 Corinthians 13:4,13 ICB)

"When we have the opportunity to help anyone, we should do it."
(Galatians 6:10 ICB)

"My children, our love should not be only words and talk. Our love must be true love. And we should show that love by what we do."
(1 John 3:18 ICB)

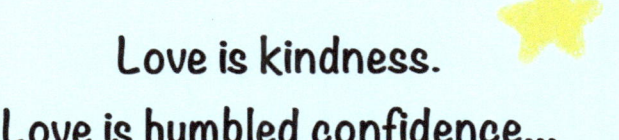

Love is kindness.
Love is humbled confidence...

Beauty sketches its reflection in invisible ink but leaves its imprint with muddy footprints on the heart.

Life is not perfect and never will be. Starting at a young age, we learn this as we face challenges. We learn that the days are not always beautiful and nothing is ever perfect. Therefore, we all make messes. We all make mistakes. However, we must teach our minds to see the beauty in the "messes" and in our imperfections because it is where we grow. We must teach our children to do the same. For their eyes and more importantly, their hearts, are always watching. We must learn, teach and believe that God loves us despite our imperfections. God loves us all through it all. And while we may not always know what to say, God is always the way. And He uses our broken parts, and our messes, for His glory.

None of us can do it alone. And yet for so many of us, spirituality seems overwhelming, and unattainable. However, that is the furthest thing from the truth and this series is a way to illustrate just that. We must teach our youth to walk with a humbled confidence that relies on the scriptures of hope and truth, instead of the ways of the world. The best part is the truth of God's word and love for us is available and waiting in everything. He accepts our broken areas and loves us anyway.

- ★ True beauty isn't found in running away from or hiding our messes, instead it is in facing and embracing them.

- ★ True beauty does not wait for perfection that will never come, but celebrates what is already here.

- ★ True beauty isn't pretending to be perfect, but empowers reality over fear.

- ★ True beauty is in celebrating imperfections, for- real not perfect- is the way.

- ★ True beauty doesn't wait for tomorrow, but learns to live for today.

- ★ True beauty is in learning to grab a hold of time even if that means agendas must wait.

- ★ True beauty knows that love can never be too late.

So step over the clutter

and laugh away the stress

for true beauty is in the art of a messy house...

so Lord, please bless this

imperfectly beautiful mess.

CPSIA information can be obtained
at www.ICGtesting.com
Printed in the USA
BVHW020218181220
595873BV00011B/46